London Borough of Tower Hamlets

91000008089764

KU-617-107

Pablo and the Noisy Party

Pablo created by Gráinne Mc Guinness

Written by Andrew Brenner and Sumita Majumdar

LADYBIRD BOOKS

UK | USA | Canada | Ireland | Australia | India | New Zealand | South Africa

Ladybird Books is part of the Penguin Random House group of companies
whose addresses can be found at global.penguinrandomhouse.com.

www.penguin.co.uk   www.puffin.co.uk   www.ladybird.co.uk

Penguin
Random House
UK

First published 2020
001

Text and illustrations copyright © Paper Owl Creative, 2020
Pablo copyright © Paper Owl Creative, 2015

PAPER OWL FILMS

Printed in China

A CIP catalogue record for this book is available from the British Library

ISBN: 978-0-241-41574-0

All correspondence to:
Ladybird Books
Penguin Random House Children's
One Embassy Gardens, New Union Square
5 Nine Elms Lane, London SW8 5DA

FSC
www.fsc.org

MIX
Paper from
responsible sources
FSC® C018179

Tang

Noa

Draff

I'm Pablo!

Llama

Mouse

Wren

These are my friends, the Book Animals!
The Book Animals live in the Art World,
where I draw my stories.

I'm going to tell you about the day my mum took me to my cousin Lorna's **birthday party**.

Mum gave me something to carry
to the party. It was a **purple box**
with a yellow ribbon around it.

I loved looking at the purple box so much
that I forgot about the party, until . . .

. . . the door opened and it got **loud!**

Suddenly I let go of the purple party box
and **ran** back to the car, where it was . . .

. . . quiet.

I found my crayons in the car
and started to draw Noasaurus
and the Art World.
"Hello, Pablo!" said Noa.

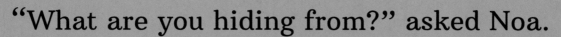

"What are you hiding from?" asked Noa.
"From the purple party box!" I said.
"What is it?" asked Noa.
"It's a party!" I told him.

"That box doesn't look like a party to me,"
said Noa. "It looks more like a **present**."
He touched the purple party box, and . . .

Noa jumped into the car to hide, too, and it was quiet again.

While we were waiting, Draff and Mouse arrived.
"Hello, Noa! Hello, Pablo!" said Draff.
"Somebody left a present here," said Mouse.

"**Stop!**" I cried.
"That's a party!" called Noa.
"A **party!**" squeaked Mouse.
"Parties are loud!"

Mouse covered her ears to hide from the
loud noises, but it was too late . . .

. . . Mouse thinking about the party had made it come back again!

LAUGHING!

TALKING!

MUSIC!

NOISE!

"Too **loud**!" cried Mouse, and she ran to the car.

"Are you scared of parties, too, Mouse?" asked Noa.
"Everybody is scared of parties," said Mouse. "Aren't they?"

"Hello, everybody!" said Tang.
"Ooh! Ooh! Are you having a party?"
"No, Tang!" I said. "We're **hiding**
from a party."
"But **why**?" asked Tang.

"Because parties can be loud," said Mouse.
"And noisy," said Noa.
"And they can get messy," said Draff.
And I said, "Parties are too full of people
who make faces I don't understand!"

I was so busy worrying about the
party that I didn't notice Wren . . .

. . . Wren was pulling at the
yellow ribbon on the purple box!
She was opening the party!

I cried out,

"NO-O-O-O-O-O-O-O-O-O-O!!"

But it was too late . . .

. . . the party present was opened
and it was surprisingly . . . quiet.

There was no loud noise. No laughing or talking or music.
"That's not the party," said Noa. "That's a toy."
"You mean a necklace," said Draff, "to be precise."
"It's a birthday present after all," said Mouse.

Suddenly, I forgot about being quiet in the car. Wren flapped and I flapped, too. Tang made up a happy song for us all to sing.

"Happy, Happy, Happy, Happy, Happy, Happy!"

"It's more like a party in **here**!" laughed Tang.
"A party is just friends getting together and having fun."
"You mean . . . **we're the party!**" said Noa.

It was fun for us, being the party in the car.
However, not everyone likes parties. Llama did
not want to go to the Art World party in the car.

"It's OK, Llama," said Mouse. "You don't have to
come to the party if you don't want to."
Llama didn't want to join us, and we all understood.

Suddenly, we noticed Mum, and the car party went quiet.
We didn't know what she was going to say.
"It's OK, Pablo," said Mum. "You don't have to go
to the party if you don't want to."

I didn't have to go to the party if I didn't want to!
Mum wrapped up the present again and I carried
it back to the house.

When the door opened, it was **loud** again!
I gave the present to Lorna, but I still didn't
want to go inside . . . but it was OK,
because I didn't have to!

Some kids like to party. Some don't, and that's OK!